The Legend of Lutey and the Merbeing

J.R.McRae

First edition, first published in Australia by Word Wings in 2016.

Text copyright ©2016 by (J.R.Poulter writing as) J.R.McRae
Illustrations copyright © by Stefania Saccarola
The moral right of the author and illustrator has been asserted.
First edition, first Australian edition 2016.
All rights reserved.
Designed by Stefania Saccarola

National Library of Australia Cataloguing-in-Publication entry
Creator: McRae, J. R., author. Title:

The legend of Lutey and the merbeing / by J.R. McRae ; illustrated by S. Saccarola.

ISBN: 9781925484137 (paperback)

Target Audience: For secondary school age.

Subjects: Fishers--Juvenile fiction.
Water spirits--Juvenile fiction.
Emotions--Juvenile fiction.
Seafaring life--Juvenile fiction.

Other Creators/Contributors: Saccarola, Stefania, illustrator.

Dewey Number: A823.3

Dedicated to my fearless son Gleeson,
[Ephesians 6:12]
J.R. McRae

Dedicated to my family,
to all my friends, maestro Franco Bressan
and the memory of my teacher and mentor Giliola.
S. Saccarola

Chapter 1 - The Singer

Matthew Trewella, 'Lutey' for his beautiful voice, used to sing the solo final hymn at Evensong in the ancient grey stone church on the Cornish coast at Zennor. His song would carry far in the evening still, its echoes lingering faintly where waves rolled in to shore. Generations of choristers had filled the little church with their singing, the wash of wind and wave carrying it down imbuing the very coves and crannies with their dulcet tones. Such songs, had the folk but known it, served more than to glory their Maker. Lutey was his mother's sole surviving son in a long line of fine voiced fishermen.

Sometimes at night he dreamed he was far out on the waves, his father's dory riding dolphin-like on the surge. He dreamed the waters swirled about the boat, holding it in a whirlpool of wild water. No matter how much he pulled and heaved at the oars, the boat was bound round. He could go neither forward nor back. He was trapped. Out of the lashing seas a shape formed, circling the boat ever closer and closer. The wind would wrap its icy fingers round him and howl in his ear. Then the very shape of his mother's fear would rise out of the water, reaching out with its long, death-cold fingers, dragging him from his boat down, down, down......

He would wake, thrashing his covers and gasping, the horrorful face large in his mind's eye. He would shudder and stare around his room but see only the wavering shadows at play on the walls. Uttering a prayer of thanks for safe-keeping, he would lie back down and sleep.

Chapter 2 - The Song

In Pendour Cove, a sea demon flowed, its spirit form like wind or breath, an 'ever presence', the something that made you shiver on a warm sunlit day. This one night, above waves whipped in frenzy by their howling riders plunging them relentlessly to shore, the sea demon heard Lutey singing. No human or spirit ever sang so sweetly! Fascinated, the spirit left the waters and came closer, the better to listen. 'Master' he breathed, 'though you controlled the songs of spheres in Paradise, you yourself could not command such song.' The one who controls the powers of the air, heard. 'Kill him', he hissed in the demon's ear.

After church, walking along the cliffs, Lutey heard a crying on the wind. He followed the sound and, to his astonishment, came upon a creature caught up on rocks above the shore. For all the world it looked like the imaginings of small boys who listen to fisher folk's tales of strange fey folk who lured their boats to doom. Now Lutey was a kind man and could not bear to see suffering. The nearer he came, the more the cryings of the creature tore at his heart. He came nearer intending to help, but the creature threw its arms around his neck and held as tight as death itself. In its bright eyes he saw the turmoil of storms and the plight of all those forever lost at sea and fearing this strange being, he thrust it from him. It fell and slipped over the cliff edge, seeming to plunge far down, down into the churning seas. Regretting his actions and fearing for its life, Lutey looked over the edge and fell.

As he hit the water and sank from sight, the dolphins who had heard his fall swam close. They nudged his limp form to the shore and swam back out to wait. The first fingers of dawn reached over the horizon, tingeing the waters with the blood of all who ever were lost at sea.

The fisher folk came at first light looking for Lutey. They did not see the sea demon leaning over, whisper in his ear,

Sing to me, sing to me,
All your long days,
Then when death claims you
Be with me always...

In a sigh of waters, the demon left...

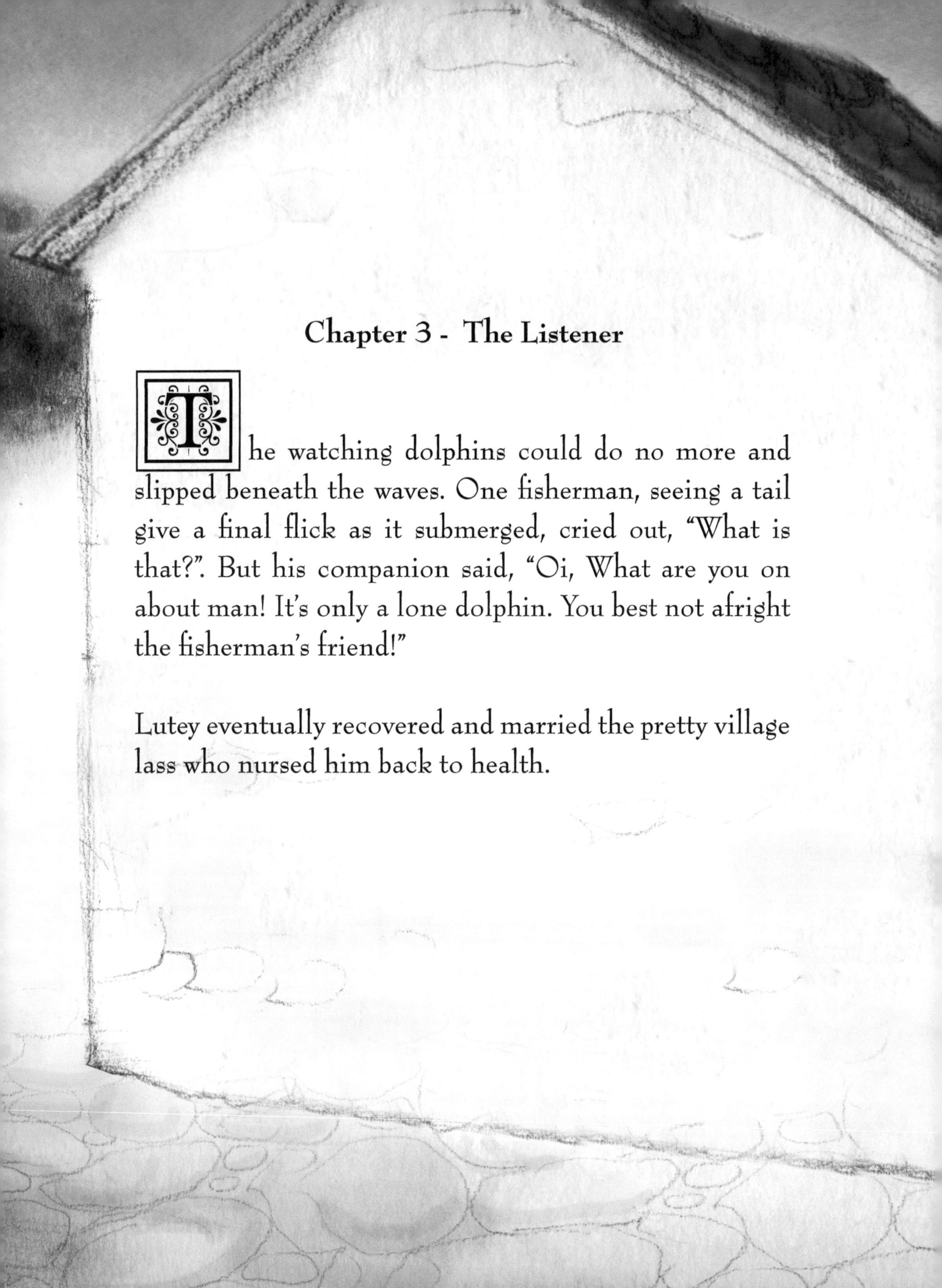

Chapter 3 - The Listener

The watching dolphins could do no more and slipped beneath the waves. One fisherman, seeing a tail give a final flick as it submerged, cried out, "What is that?". But his companion said, "Oi, What are you on about man! It's only a lone dolphin. You best not afright the fisherman's friend!"

Lutey eventually recovered and married the pretty village lass who nursed him back to health.

Sometimes, he would wake at night in their cottage high on the cliffs and say to his wife, "Hist, can you hear it? Someone is crying, we must go see!" But his wife would always calm him, "Nay Lutey love, come back to sleep, it is only the wild wind in the caverns on shore." Lutey would lie back down and sleep. And nothing the sea demon could do would draw him forth, for of course, it was the deceiver's voice that cried in the wind.

Years passed. Lutey and his wife led the lives of good folk, respected by their community, and never turned away anyone who needed help.

Lutey still sang in the church, his beautiful, strong voice floating out over the village and across the cliffs to the sea. Far off, the sea demon would drift on the surface and listen till the last note drifted away into silence. Then he would whisper to himself,

Sing to me, sing to me,
E'en tho' it grieves me,
Then when death claims you,
You'll never leave me...

The sea demon longed to draw the song from Lutey's throat and silence him forever. But he had not the power of life and death so he could only wait....

Chapter 4 - Crescendo

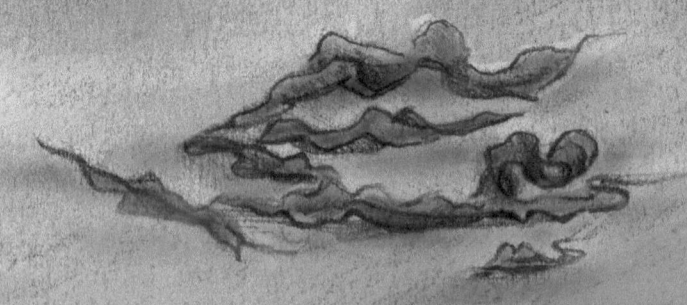 ow Lutey never did go fishing with the other men. Instead he found, after his near drowning that he seemed to know the secrets of the kelp gardens. When the fisherfolk brought their nets ashore with the long strands of kelp weed entangled or when it was washed up ashore after a storm, Lutey would harvest it and turn it into ointments and remedies, the fame of which spread through all the isles.

One day, when he was a very old man and his hair as grey as the winter sky, he stood on the cliff edge and started singing , softly, then louder and louder till all his ebbing strength was taken up in the song. As the last note left his throat, Lutey felt a surge in the air around him, and a presence pull him towards the cliff edge and the now swirling turmoil of wind and water below. Lutey struggled for all his life depended on it. His cries for help were caught by the demon seething round him and muffled in the oncoming roar of storm. The ragged rocks huddled along the shore reached through the waves a plea. For even rocks cry out when all other voices are still. Only the dolphins heard but had no power to help.

As he fought, Lutey felt one last song stir deep in his soul and cried out, "Though I die, yet will I see my Maker!" and he sang from the oldest pages in the Book of Life a song of eternal struggle and infinite peace. The more he sang the stronger his voice and the sea demon hissing and lashing around the old man could not reckon with the force of the words.

Finally, the demon let go of Lutey and slid away into the depths.

Chapter 5 - Finale

Lutey lay on the cliff edge, all his strength was gone. His wife, winding her way down the path from their cottage found him. He smiled at her, 'It is alright love, it is not time yet. Wait with me a while, my strength is spent.' The fisher folk helped her take Lutey back to his cottage. He lived long enough to bless his children and whilst they sang, he slipped gently into his Maker's keeping.

The sea demon tormented by his loss, had sought that he might yet take Lutey to his Master. But, when he sensed Lutey's spirit leave, he gnashed at the air and tore at the rocks, ripping the very boulders from the cliff. With all his might he sought to take the very cottage from the cliff and tumble all within to their doom. But even as he hurled the waves, the very waters heard the words of the children's song,

"In the midst of turmoil of wind and wave
The Lord said, "Peace, be still"
And the very seas and winds obeyed
Their Maker's will.

The seas subsided and the wind lulled. Everything was still...

Zennor has a Mermaid's Rock where, it is said, the sea creature tried to lure Matthew Trewella, Lutey, to his death.

The End

Author

J.R.Poulter once worked in a circus. This definitely qualifies her to write for children! Published in **Australia**, UK, USA and Europe, she has over 30 children's and education books with mainstream & digital publishers. Major awards, include Children's Choice, NZ, inclusion in Top Ten Children's & YA Books, NZ and Premier's Recommended Reading List, NSW. More books are coming. J.R. loves teaching fun with words and doing dramatised book readings. She created a **picture book in collaboration with Craig Smith, for a participatory audience at the Lockyer Festival.** Under J.R.McRae, she creates novels (including YA), award winning **literary poetry, short stories** and artworks. Her current adventure consists of global collaborations with other gifted creatives.

http://www.jenniferrpoulter.weebly.com/
http://www.jrmcrae_subversive.weebly.com
www.wordwings.wix.com/publishing

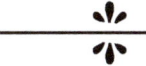

Illustrator

Stefania Saccarola is an illustrator and a graphic designer. She contributed to the Cabo Verde Natura 2000 project, organized by Las Palmas University (Spain), creating illustrations of native fauna. In 2002, she was selected by the International Illustrators Exhibition, part of the Bologna Children's Book Fair (Italy), and her work was published in the Annual 2002 Non Fiction. In 2003, she contributed some illustrations to The Encyclopedia of Mammals - McRae Books.

She worked for a couple of years in a television program for children, live-illustrating fairy tales for children. She continues to create illustrations and paintings, while working as a graphic designer.

http://www.chimeradesign.it
http://www.disegnetti.blogspot.it